Nighty Night, Baby Jesus

A Noisy Nativity

By

Molly Schaar Idle

Abingdon Press
Nashville

Library of Congress Cataloging-in-Publication Data

Idle, Molly Schaar.
  Nighty night, Baby Jesus : a noisy Nativity / by Molly Schaar Idle.
      p. cm.
  Summary: Rhyming text tells of stable animals awakening to find a baby boy in their manger, and raising their voices joyfully until Mary asks them to hush so that Jesus can sleep.
  ISBN 978-1-4267-0030-9 (binding: hardback/picture book, casebound : alk. paper) 1. Jesus Christ—Nativity—Juvenile fiction. [1. Stories in rhyme. 2. Jesus Christ—Nativity—Fiction. 3. Animal sounds—Fiction.] I. Title.

PZ8.3.I1372Nig 2009
[E]—dc22

                                  2008049773

                    09 10 11 12 13 14 15 16 17—10 9 8 7 6 5 4 3 2 1

                              Printed in China

For Steve

and

our baby boys from heaven

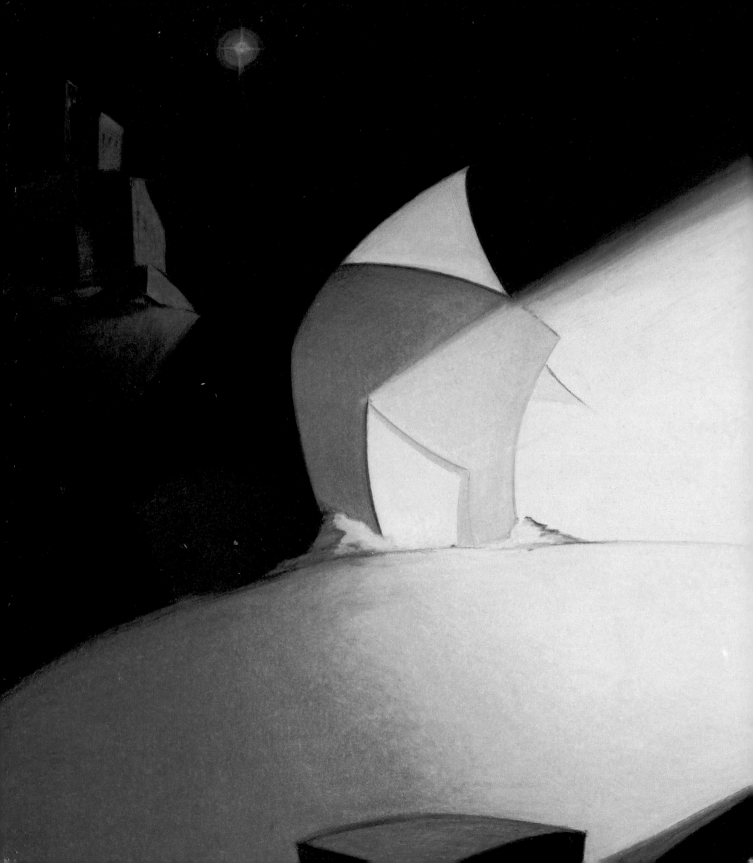

One night in sleepy Bethlehem
    a single star shone down,
illuminating miracles
    below in that small town.

Outside the silent stable
    all was dark that holy night.
But, rising from the manger
    came the Son's warm, glowing light.

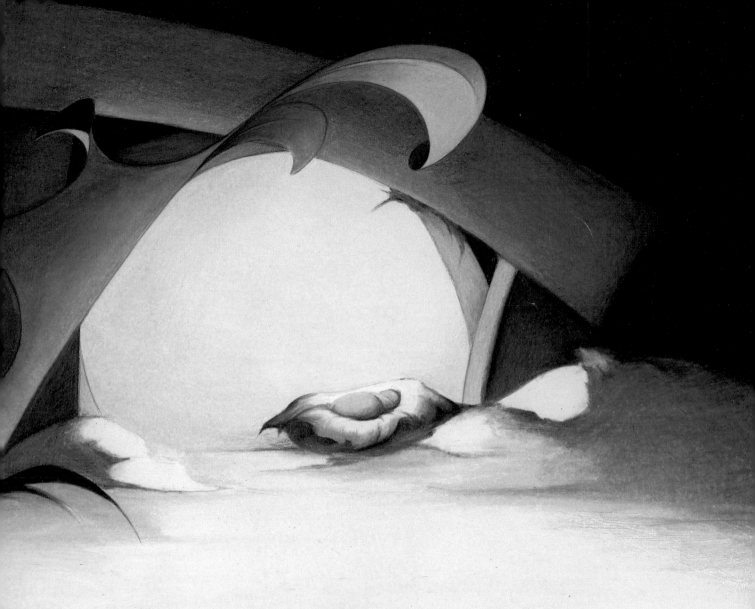

So bright it woke the Rooster,
  who thought day had come anew.
He crowed to wake the animals with
  "COCK-A-DOODLE-DO!"

Up for work, the Ox plowed toward
his breakfast in the manger.
But, in place of food, he found
a perfect Little Stranger.

The Ox was taken by surprise
and sounded a low

"MOO."

This roused the Cow and her small Calf,
who sounded their "MOO" too.

On wobbly legs, the Calf set out
to find some hay to graze.
Then face to face and nose to nose,
she met the Baby's gaze.

This struck the Donkey funny,
and he laughed at what he saw—

threw back his head, kicked up his heels,
and burst out with "HEE-AW!"

The Camel, taking in the scene,
    watched as the Donkey brayed.
Then, wisely, knelt before the crib,
    and *silently* she prayed.

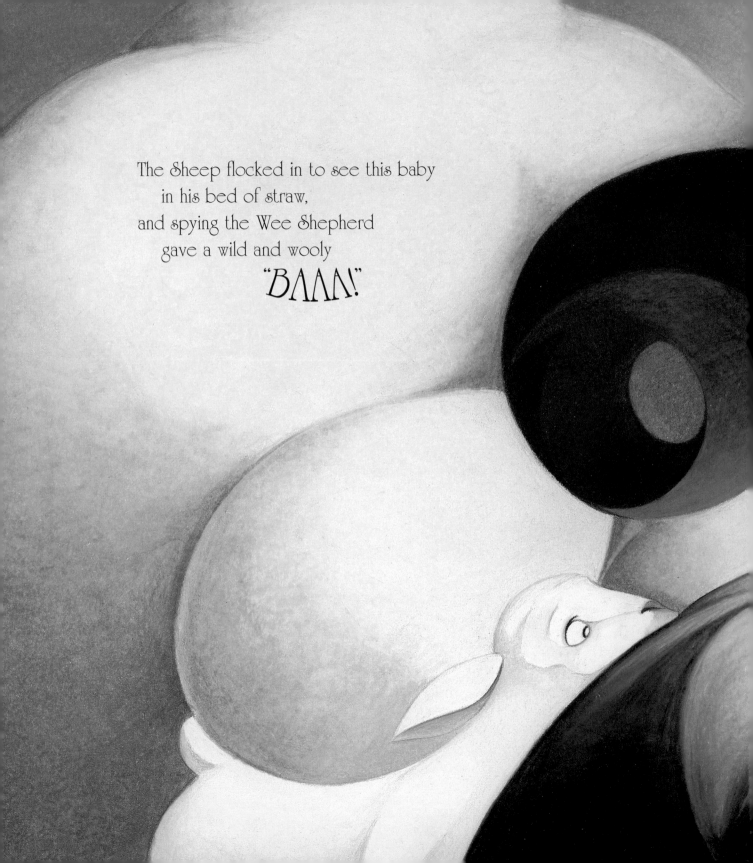

The Sheep flocked in to see this baby
in his bed of straw,
and spying the Wee Shepherd
gave a wild and wooly
"BAAA!"

The Goat heard all the ruckus
and came in to have his say.
His mouth was full as usual,
but he "MAΛΛ℮d" anyway.

And then, the Hen with Chicks in tow,
    came in to take a peep.
All standing up on tiny toes,
    they chorused
        CHEEP! CHEEP! CHEEP!

The Dog came in and joined the rest,
    he wagged from end to end.
This Little Boy in swaddling clothes
    was sure to be a friend.

He chased the chickens round about
    and barked a joyous "WOOF!"

And it was this that woke the Cat
    so lazily aloof.

    She yawned and stretched, and unimpressed,
        prepared to bathe her fur.
    But then a tiny hand, so soft,
    reached up and made her
        "PURRRRRRRR."

From "COCK-A-DOODLE-DO"
to "PURRRRRRRR,"
each made a joyful sound.
Until, with Mary's gentle "Shhh . . ."
a hush fell all around.

His mother picked him up
    and cooed a gentle lullaby.
Her Baby Boy from heaven yawned
    and closed his sleepy eyes.

"Sweet dreams," she whispered softly,
    precious bundle in her lap.
Time for her Son to settle down
    and have a little nap.

Nighty night, sweet Baby Jesus,
    all is calm, all is bright,
while up above the star shines down—
    your heavenly night-light.

Nighty Night, Baby Jesus.